D0363868

Little Bear's Alphabet

JANE HISSEY

HUTCHINSON

London Sydney Auckland Johannesburg

a b c d e f g h i j k l m

A is for animals. All the animals are asleep
except Little Bear.

B b

B is for box. Bramwell Brown has a big box
of buttons.

C c

C is for cake. Bramwell is cutting a piece for Camel.

Dd

D is for doll. She is wearing a blue dress and hat.

Ee

E is for egg. Be extra careful, Little Bear.
Please don't drop it.

Ff

F is for food. This picnic food looks fun to eat.

G g

G is for game. The toys are playing a game of hide-and-seek. Can you find them?

Hh

H is for holding on. Hold on tight, Little Bear,
Hoot is flying high.

a b c d e f g h i j k l m

I i

I is for inside. Little Bear is inside his sleeping bag.

J j

J is for jelly. Don't jump in Ruff's birthday jelly,
Little Bear.

a b c d e f g h i j k l m

K k

K is for kangaroo. She is kicking a big red ball.

L l

L is for leaf. Don't let go, Little Bear.

Mm

M is for marbles. How many marbles has Cat found?

Nn

N is for nest. Hoot's new nest is a nice woolly hat.

O o

O is for on. Old Bear is sitting on top of a basket watching Little Bear.

P p

P is for present. This one is wrapped in pretty paper.

Q q

Q is for quiet please. Old Bear is sleeping under his quilt.

R r

R is for run. Rabbit is running in a race.

S s

S is for sand, small stones and a spade.

Tt

T is for tent. These two friends are camping
in the garden.

a b c d e f g h i j k l m

U u

U is for upside down. There are four bricks under
Little Bear.

V v

V is for vase. That's not a very good hiding
place, Rabbit!

Ww

W is for wool. I wonder what Bramwell Brown is knitting?

X x

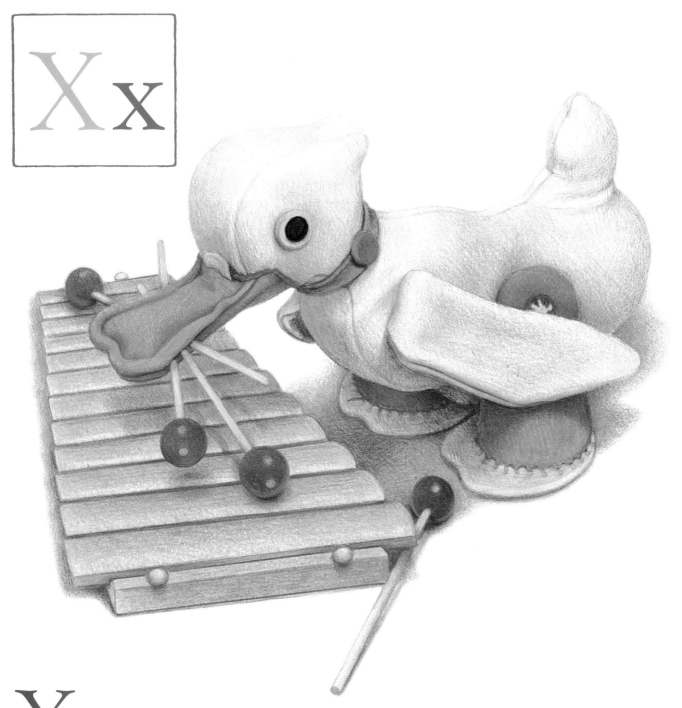

X is for xylophone. Duck is playing some music.

a b c d e f g h i j k l m

Yy

Y is for yellow. Can you see two yellow ducks?

Z z

Z is for Zebra. What is she pulling in her little red cart?

Some letters make new sounds
when they are side by side.

Sh

Th

ch

Ch

th

sh

Ch

Ch is for choose. Little Bear has chosen a chalk to write with.

Sh

Sh is for shadows. Little Bear is showing Rabbit his shadow picture on the wall.

Th

Th is for things. What letters do the things on the shelves begin with?

For Di

First published in 2000

3 5 7 9 10 8 6 4 2

Text and Illustrations © copyright Jane Hissey 1986, 1987, 1988,
1989, 1990, 1992, 1994, 1996, 1999, 2000

Jane Hissey has asserted her right under
the Copyright, Designs and Patents Act, 1988,
to be identified as the author and illustrator of this work

First published in the United Kingdom in 2000 by
Hutchinson Children's Books
The Random House Group Limited
20 Vauxhall Bridge Road, London SW1V 2SA

Random House Australia (Pty) Limited
20 Alfred Street, Milsons Point, Sydney
New South Wales 2061, Australia

Random House New Zealand Limited
18 Poland Road, Glenfield
Auckland 10, New Zealand

Random House South Africa (Pty) Limited
Endulini, 5A Jubilee Road, Parktown 2193, South Africa

The Random House Group Limited Reg. No. 954009

www.randomhouse.co.uk

A CIP catalogue record for this book is available from the British Library

ISBN: 0 09 176907 8

Printed in Singapore